the MYSTERY of the MEANEST TEACHER

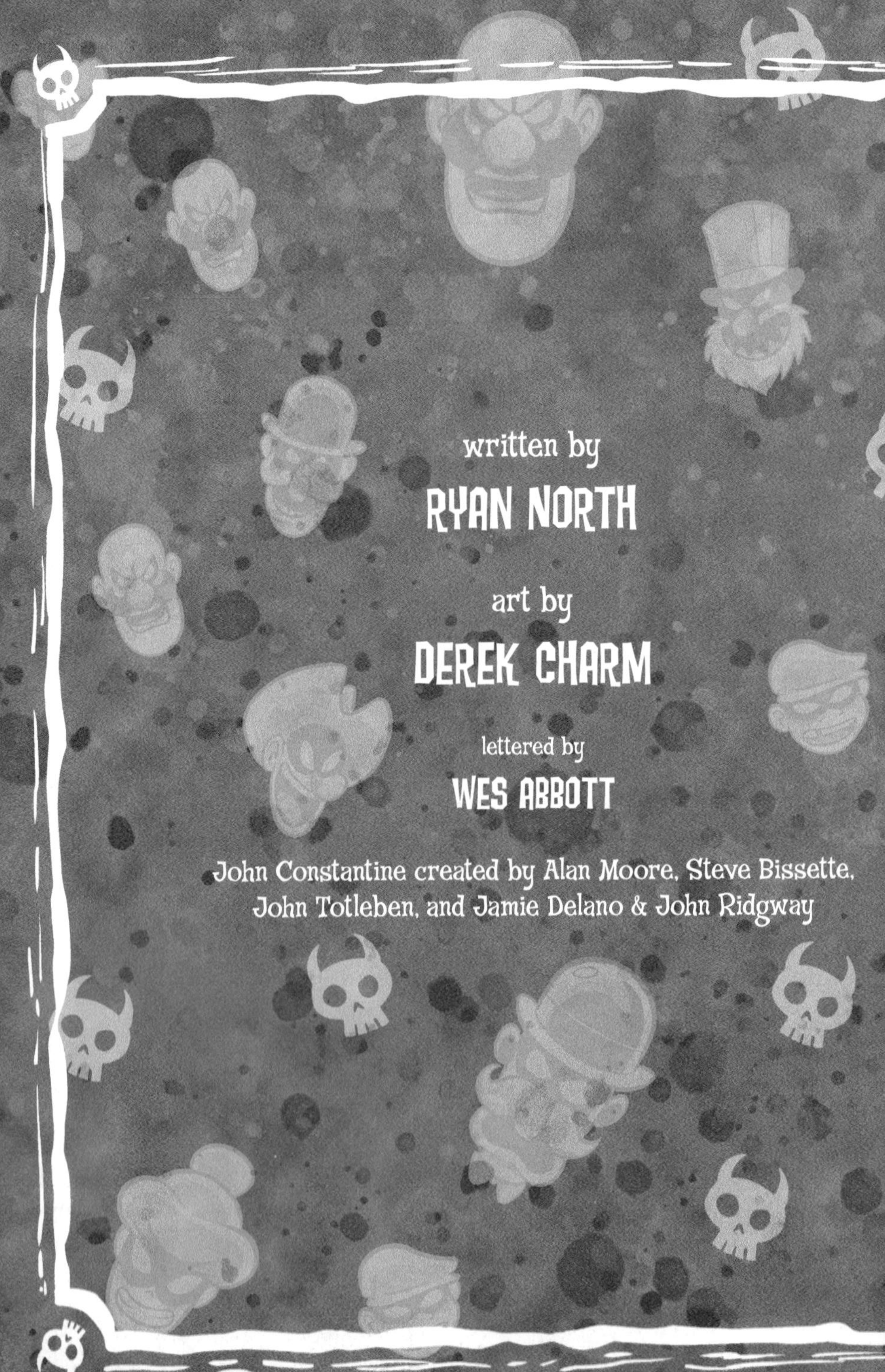

written by

RYAN NORTH

art by

DEREK CHARM

lettered by

WES ABBOTT

John Constantine created by Alan Moore, Steve Bissette, John Totleben, and Jamie Delano & John Ridgway

the MYSTERY of the MEANEST TEACHER

a JOHNNY CONSTANTINE graphic novel

JIM CHADWICK Editor
DIEGO LOPEZ Associate Editor
STEVE COOK Design Director - Books
AMIE BROCKWAY-METCALF Publication Design
TIFFANY HUANG Publication Production

MARIE JAVINS Editor-in-Chief, DC Comics

DANIEL CHERRY III Senior VP - General Manager
JIM LEE Publisher & Chief Creative Officer
JOEN CHOE VP - Global Brand & Creative Services
DON FALLETTI VP - Manufacturing Operations & Workflow Management
LAWRENCE GANEM VP - Talent Services
ALISON GILL Senior VP - Manufacturing & Operations
NICK J. NAPOLITANO VP - Manufacturing Administration & Design
NANCY SPEARS VP - Revenue

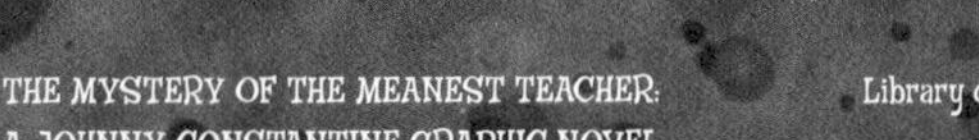

THE MYSTERY OF THE MEANEST TEACHER:
A JOHNNY CONSTANTINE GRAPHIC NOVEL

DC Comics, 2900 West Alameda Ave., Burbank, CA 91505
Printed by LSC Communications, Crawfordsville, IN, USA. 5/21/21.
First Printing.
ISBN: 978-1-77950-123-3

Library of Congress Cataloging-in-Publication Data

Names: North, Ryan, 1980- writer. | Charm, Derek, artist. | Abbott, Wes, letterer.
Title: The mystery of the meanest teacher : a Johnny Constantine graphic novel / written by Ryan North ; art by Derek Charm ; lettered by Wes Abbott.
Description: Burbank, CA : DC Comics, [2021] | "John Constantine created by Alan Moore, Steve Bissette, John Totleben, and Jamie Delano & John Ridgway" | Audience: Ages 8-12 | Audience: Grades 4-6 | Summary: After angering a number of hostile spirits in England, thirteen-year-old magician John Constantine is sent to the Junior Success Boarding School in Salem, Massachusetts where he and fellow misfit Anna try to find out if their teacher Ms. Kayla is a witch.
Identifiers: LCCN 2021004933 (print) | LCCN 2021004934 (ebook) | ISBN 9781779501233 (paperback) | ISBN 9781779508591 (ebook)
Subjects: LCSH: Graphic novels. | CYAC: Graphic novels. | Fantasy. | Magic--Fiction. | Witches--Fiction. | Demonology--Fiction.
Classification: LCC PZ7.7.N6756 My 2021 (print) | LCC PZ7.7.N6756 (ebook)
| DDC 741.5/973--dc23
LC record available at https://lccn.loc.gov/2021004933
LC ebook record available at https://lccn.loc.gov/2021004934

TABLE OF CONTENTS

To all the Kid Constantines out there.

—Ryan and Derek

This.
This is the best candy store in the universe.
ARCHIBALD JUNIOR'S DISCOUNT CONFECTIONS
Chapter One:
In which our hero...
In which our champion...
In which our protagonist is met.

But I'm not anyone else.

GUMMY BEARS

I'm Johnny. Only my dad's a John too, so folks call me "Kid." Kid Constantine.

And I'm the only one in the world who knows magic.

Auxilio tuo, oblique nunc pergo.

GUMMY BEARS

Real magic.

Which makes me the greatest magician in the world, mate.

GUMMY SCARES
There we go. Nice 'n' easy.
Take a step sideways into the ghost realm, and you'll find Grandpa Archibald's Olde-Tyme Candy Confectionery.
It's hidden in a separate dimension on top of the "real" Archibald's.

Old Man Archibald's a ghost. He's been dead for centuries.

Didn't stop him from opening up his new shop and getting better at what he does every single day for a few hundred years straight.

And now his chocolate bars, well...

They're to die for.
Hey! Stop right there!
Take one more bite and I'll make sure YOU turn into a ghost, too!

Arphibalph! Glud du schee yo!
A smarter specimen would swallow before he speaks, boy.

CHEW
CHEW
CHEW

GULP!

CHOMP!
CONSTANTINE!

Now Archibald, your chocolate is just too irresistible. If anything I'm the victim here, so—
Save it for the living, kid. That sweet talk won't work on me.
You're a thief.
"Thief"? Please. "Charming rogue," perhaps, but—
It might've still been cute when you were eight, John, but this really has to—
Stop...
You fool. You didn't.
Those chocolates were the only things standing between our world and complete destruction, Constantine!
Wait wait wait! Calm down! I can explain!
Well? Nobody's stopping you, boy!
Okay, the one thing you need to know is, um...
I'm real sorry?
Idiot. There are forces at play here that you can't even fathom.
Whoa! Hey!
You're gonna get a long-overdue education, Johnny.

"At the center of the Earth slumbers Nappi'loth, the **slumbering** and **nameless** god of **madness** and **chaos!**"
"I thought you said she was nameless."
"She **is** nameless! Nappi'loth is just what **I** call her, on account of how she doesn't have a name!
"Every decade she awakens, ready to destroy the world, and the **only** things that even just **delay** her destruction...
"Are the **eternal chocolates.**
"After she eats them, she falls back into a slumber—which allows **us,** both living and ghosts, another decade of existence!
"It's the **only** way we've held back destruction for **generations!**
And you just **gobbled** one, Kid! Now she'll only sleep for eight years, tops!

So make another one! You're the best, I'm sure—
Even with my skill, they take years to craft! That's why they're called the Eternal Chocolates.
You've just messed up my schedule for the next five years, Constantine!
Look, I said I was sorry, so let's not do something we'll all regret...
Oh, I'm very certain I'm not going to regret this at all...
Archibald! Listen, Archibald! You—you...
You've got chocolate to make! You'd better get busy chocolatiering and let me go, right?
You may be half right: I do need to get to work, thanks to you.
But as for the other half...
Cousins! Your services are required! You were right all along about Constantine: he IS a little jerk!
Archibald! Buddy! Remember all the good times we've had and—
I won't stop you anymore, cousins! Now's your chance!

Hah! What's the matter, Constantine?
You look like you've seen a **ghost.**

Right. Ghost dinosaurs.
I didn't know there was such a thing as ghost dinosaurs.
Hic murus est mihi trans-grediendus, facias portam quaeso!

So this one's on me.

Of **course** ghost animal trainers would want to train a ghost animal like that.
Auxilio tuo, oblique nunc pergo! **Auxilio tuo, oblique nunc pergo!**
Of **course** they'd turn them into the greatest hunters the afterlife has ever known.

It makes sense. And that's bad news for me.

I do my best work when things **don't** make sense.
Get **off the road!**
Where'd he **come** from?
HONNK!
HONNK!

So now if I want to stay alive, all I've got to do is escape a dinosaur I can't even **see** anymore.
What are you doing, you reckless kid?
No sweat.

Lucky for me, I've become friendly with some local demons.
Igmal! Sangrath! Exaudite me! Exaudite meam precem!

And being friendly with demons...
Johnny Constantine...

It has its **advantages.**
You really are a right ***idiot.***

Close the portal, Igmal! The ghosts, they're after me! They'll—
They'll not be able to reach you **here,** my little acquaintance. I can promise you that much.

But they **will** nab you when you return to your world.
You'll be safe there during the day, but the second night arrives...
I know, I know, I'll be hunted by an army of cheesed-off ghost men and women and dinosaurs—

And ghost men and women **on** dinosaurs—

All of whom can walk through walls.
I warned you about irritating the ghosts, Kid.
Ah, I'll figure something out. I always do.

I don't think you will. Ghosts have long memories, John. You won't be able to talk your way out of this one.

Okay, *fine.* So instead I'll spend my days in my world *as usual,* and just come visit *you* three every night to sleep.
Suits me fine! You demons are fun!

It'll be like a sleepover. We'll cuddle up by the infernal *flames,* roast *marshmallows,* maybe swap a few *secrets...*
Johnny.
You don't think your *parents* will notice your absence?

Right.
My *parents.*

Where's Johnny, sweetie?
He said he was just going out for some snacks...

I *could* send a shambling replica to take your place tonight—
Thanks, Igmal! I owe you one.
I will decrease the count of the favors we owe you accordingly, Constantine.

Mother. Father. I have returned.
Ah, hey, John. Just in time for bed.

Yes. I now go to my bedroom to spend eight hours unconscious, as is the custom of our species, of all living flesh.
We all agree this is normal, do we not, fellow humans?
There's my boy.

..

So that "fellow humans" bit is new.
Ah.
You know kids. Probably saw it in some video online.

I cannot sustain this Constantine construct indefinitely.
Come on—it'll just be for a few nights, tops!
And as *I* have already told you, ghosts do not forget.

Nah. You worry too much.
Mark my words, Igmal: three nights from now, everything will be back to normal.

The first night, my sleepover plan worked great...
He stinks like human.
Oh yes, you may be able to craft **mines,** hero, but can you craft...**love?**

Even on the fifth night...
That **couch** and **mortal food** he brought here **also** stink like human. Where'd you find this kid?
It *is* pretty noticeable...
Oh yes, this isn't the world of **Peace**craft you're used to, hero! Quite the **opposite...**

But everyone's luck runs out eventually. Especially mine.
ENOUGH! It's been **ten nights,** Constantine!
Oh no, look at all these animals crossing here! If only someone could supply them with **mortgages...**
HECK BLAZER

Okay okay okay, *I hear you.* I thought the ghosts would forget, and they didn't. But I have a new plan: ***America.***
My parents suggested it at breakfast.

There's this boarding school there—and all I have to do is say yes and I can be on a plane ***this week.***

It solves everything! I go where ***nobody*** knows me while the heat dies down here, plus I'm out of your hair! Horns. Whatever!
That...actually ***would*** solve everything. Huh.

You're going to say yes and go, right?
I figure. Parents cramp my style, you know?
Yes, you should definitely leave right away.

Sangrath, do I detect ***your*** infernal fingerprints on this scheme?
Mayyyyyyyybe.

Please send Johnny away to boarding school in America, ***please*** send Johnny away to boarding school in America, ***please send Johnny away to boarding school in America...***

My mates helped me pack the next morning.
So what do you know about Massachusetts?
Nothin'. Figure I don't need to.
HECK BLA

I'm ***Kid Constantine***— I can go ***anywhere*** and land on my feet! I won't know anyone there, and that's how I like it.
Sure thing, Kid.
Okay, I think you're all packed now, byeee!
HECK BLAZER

Although...hey, I just had a crazy idea! How about ***you*** guys come with me?
Come with you...?
To school! To ***America!***

We could have lots of fun pranking my new classmates! What d'you say?
DEVIL
HECK BLAZER
Oh, uh...

I don't do well in small spaces?
Yeah, and *uh*...oh! They serve salted pretzels on planes and we demons have a weakness to salt!
That's actually true! Better safe than sorry, that's what I always say!

Come on, mates! Come with me! It'll be **fun.**
Johnny...
Oh my **gosh,** Igmal. **I'll** tell him.

Johnny. **Listen** to me. We are **not**—
—and we never **will** be—
—your **mates.**

Yeah, you did us some favors once and we did you some in return. That's not **friendship.** That's just **business,** kid.
We don't want to **travel** with you. We want to be **rid** of you.

Right. I know what you're thinking here, too...
Ouch. Sucks to be me.

Only it **doesn't** suck. Not really.
I've had friends before...
So I know the truth about friendship...

You ever wonder what things would be like if magic was *real,* Johnny?
Um...
This is Ben. My first and last "best friend."

He was special, and I liked him a lot. So much that I decided to share a secret with him that I'd never told *anyone.*
What would you say if I told you *I* knew magic?
Hah! Yeah right. I'd laugh.
People talk about magic like it's real, but it's not.
It's just adults pretending.
Like fairies and monsters.

Nobody knows magic. Not *real* magic.
Ben...

That's just not true anymore.

AHHHHHHHHH!

It was horrible.
HELP! JOHNNY'S A MONSTER! JOHNNY'S A DISGUSTING—
Ben! **Wait!**

HELP! ANYONE! JOHNNY'S A DEMON!
Ben was afraid of me. He was **disgusted** by me. He was about to **reveal** me. I did the only thing I could...
Vocem oboedientiae invoco!

I cast a spell of obedience, and asked him to forget everything he knew that was weird about me.
Ben, I want you to forget everything you know that's weird about me, okay?

Ben?
...

I'm sorry, I don't know you and my mom doesn't like it when I talk to strangers.
And my best friend since year one forgot me **entirely.**

Because you'll never get hurt again.

Oh yeah, I mean, that's how I prefer it too, for sure. Lone wolf. I was just trying to be polite, you know?
That's actually my one rule: ***never*** get too close to ***anyone.***

Okay, bye everyone, get out of here, I don't need you and you don't need me so there's no need for us to hang out!
Farewell, Johnny.
Yep. Smell you later!

HECK BLAZER

Smell ***you*** later too, entire British Empire.
And as for you, America: ready or not—
HECK BLAZER

UNACCOMPANIED
MINOR
PLEASE ENSURE I AM
DELIVERED TO GATE 15

15

Here I come.

JUNIOR SUCCESS BOARDING SCHOOL
Ah, the joys of being the weird new kid who arrives partway through the school year.
There's nothing like it.
Chapter Two:
In which our other protagonist is met...
Because we have two of them...
So already this book is giving you value.

Love to not know where anything is.

Love to get picked last in everything.

Love to get the half-broken desk nobody else wanted.

But you know Mr. Hoover's gym class...!
Breakfast for dinner!
Love to be surrounded by inscrutable in-jokes just because I'm the one kid who missed the first few weeks of school.

Excuse me, is this Ms. Bravo's math class?
Anyone?
And again, and I cannot stress this enough...

Each of us has a **relationship** with our body, and that relationship can **change** over time. There's no right or wrong—
GIRLS: Your changing body
Yes? Can I help you?
Uh...
The Heart
Love to not know where anything is.

I'm looking for Ms. Bravo's math class, love?

No, you will call me Mrs. Barkley. Ms. Bravo's class is in room 204 **East.** You're in 204 West.
I'm afraid you're in the completely wrong wing.
Unless, of course, you've come here to learn about your changing female body?

Hah hah is that the new kid?
Oh my *god.*
Did he call her "love"? *Ahhhhh* he's such a ***loser!***

No sorry bye.

Also: love to discover how much I'd been relying on my anti-blushing spell at the **same** time I discover most of my spells don't even **work** here.
Different continent, different rules. Just another surprise America had for me.

Just having a completely fun and normal day here in Massachusetts.

Ah, you must be young Johnny Constantine.
Kid. Call me Kid.
Fair enough.

Find yourself a seat, Kid.
READ

Oh my gosh *haha* look he's gonna sit next to ***Anna!***
It's game over for New Kid before he even ***meets*** anyone! It's so ***sad!***

Hey.
Hey.

So we were looking at the Pythagorean theorem.

As we saw, it only applies to right triangles...
Come on, pencil, where are you...?

But we've seen that *any* non-right triangle can be reduced into... anyone?
I don't believe this...

Two right triangles?
That's correct, Anna.
First day of school, and I'm already risking public magic. Terrific.

Aerem in peniculum nunc compono.
It's a lesser summoning spell, but at least it's not **completely** broken. The pencil's not the greatest...

But I'm just trying to get through the day here.

So, as with anything in mathematics...

You shouldn't believe anything until you can prove it.

Luckily for you, there are over 300 different ways to prove the Pythagorean theorem.

Let's start with an easy one...

So my first day was the worst, and it's not over yet. Turns out we get a free period before dinner. Everyone meets their friends and plays games.
Three guesses who's not invited to join.
I don't mind. It gives me time to think. **Brooding** gets a—
Johnny!
As I was saying, brooding gets a—
Hey, Johnny!
It gets a bad rap, but it's—
Wait up!
Can't you see I'm **trying** to **think?!**

Seems like you're more focused on trying to be a loner, but sure. Cool. You're trying to think.
I'll think with you.

Listen—it's Anna, right?
Right. And you're the new kid. Johnny "the Kid" Constantine.

Just *Kid.* Anna, I'd really rather you left me alone. I'm not looking to make friends, okay?
That's great, because nobody here wants to be friends with me, either. You'll fit in fine.

No, you don't understa—
In fact, I'm pretty sure the only reason my parents sent me here is that they *also* didn't know what to do with me.

Grade six is all about fitting in, and I don't. And that's *fine.* I'm not changing who I am, and if that's the price, then I don't *want* to fit in.
So if you're not talking to me because of that, well—it's nothing I haven't dealt with before, Kid.

Great. Well, that's sorted, and I'll just—
Nuh-uh. Not so fast. Before you run off to be all dark and broody, there's something you need to do.

You need to tell me ***exactly*** how you pulled a pencil out of ***thin air*** in Ms. Bravo's class.

I have no idea what you're talking about.
I—I just took it out of my bag. I was fast, maybe you didn't—
Nope. Don't lie to me, Kid. I know what I saw.
You said something in Greek and a pencil appeared in your hand, like—like you ***summoned*** it.
Well. I suppose there's no point hiding anymore, Anna.
You've figured it out, and you deserve the truth.

My name's ***Johnny the Magnificent...***
And I do ***magic tricks.***

And that wasn't Greek, it was Latin. When real magicians do a trick, they're always talking. It's called "patter"—keeps people distracted.
So I do it, too.

It's a hobby. And magicians are never supposed to reveal their secrets, but—it really wasn't that impressive, Anna. Just some sleight of hand.
Had the pencil hidden up my sleeve the whole time.

Kid Constantine...

That is the **coolest** thing I've ever heard!

I can't believe ***you*** like magic! I like magic, too!
Yeah, I—
I tried magic books, but they're all baby tricks, you know?
Trick shuffles and dummy coins. It's all I can find! Do you have any magic books?

No, it's— it's just a hobby. Self-taught. Anyway— I really gotta go, Anna.
Can I show you one of my tricks before you go? I'm getting good, Johnny, I promise. I just need to say the magic words...

I don't see any trick. What are you...?
It takes a second.

Now. Like I said, Johnny: I'm getting good at magic.
And I'm ***easily*** good enough to know what you did in class ***was*** real.

Look, Anna, I don't know what you ***think*** you saw, but it was just a stupid trick, a—
No, it ***wasn't.*** Why are you ***lying*** to me?
I'm not lying!
Why are you so certain that I'm lying?

Because, Johnny...
You're not the only kid around here with a few *tricks* up their sleeve.
SNAP!

clink
clink
clink

What are you—
Shh!

It seems I have your attention, Kid Constantine.

I thought I was the only one. I've never met anyone else who knows magic. Real magic.
Same.

I always thought I was alone—
Same, Kid. **Same.** I think we have a lot in common.
I think we should be friends.

Oh no, no, I have a rule against friends, I—
And I have a rule against making friends with annoying jerks who lie to me.
But I'm gonna bend it for you, okay?

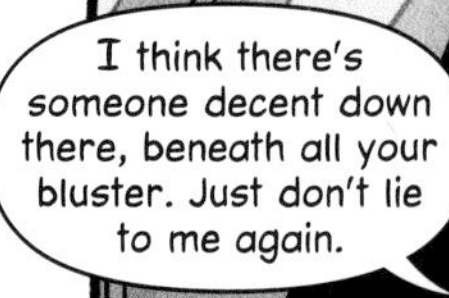
I think there's someone decent down there, beneath all your bluster. Just don't lie to me again.

Plus, we're the only two magic kids in the universe. **Come on.** We can't **not** know each other.

So.
Friends?

I know, I **know.** It's risky. I shouldn't do it. I'm gonna get hurt.
Friends.
But rules **were** meant to be broken...

And I don't think Anna would take no for an answer anyway.

We can stop shaking any time now, Johnny.
Right! Right.

So, Kid...
What other tricks do you know?

Aerem in peniculum nunc compono.

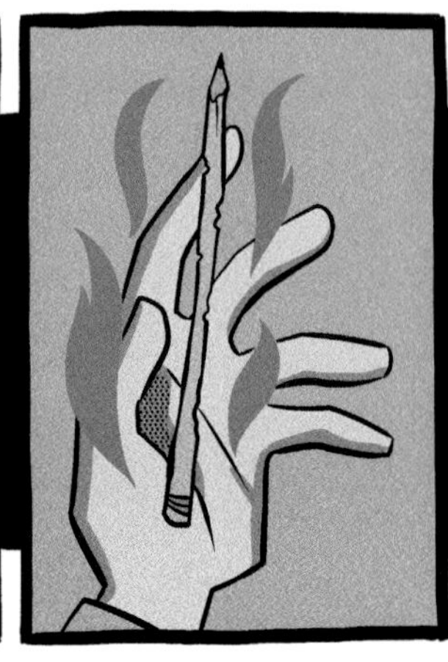

Teacher's Lounge
This takes more effort for larger locks, but...
Muta statum pessuli.

Ready?
Ready.

Tibi nunc impero ut magnitudine excrescas.

Aerem in peniculum nunc compono.

klik

Oh, I am gonna **use** that.

crrt?

Hey, what are you looking a—
NOTHING! GO AWAY PLEASE!

Weirdos.

Back in England that ant'd be the size of a lorry.
My spells don't work as well in America though. Maybe it's something about ley lines, or—
It's awesome. This is incredible.
Well, the ***really*** incredible spells actually summon demons—no big deal for me—but they only work on European ones. They don't do anything here.
Look, the least I can do is teach you one of my spells in exchange.
The levitation spell? Ooh, yes please!
It only works on things that are already light, but—okay. You don't use Latin though. You just whisper like this...
Give it a shot.
Try and stop me.
DINING HALL
Brilliant.
That's right and proper ***brilliant.***

Lemonade, love. On the rocks.
Uh-huh.

And for you?
Water's fine, thanks.

I've never done stuff like this in public before. I can't believe nobody's noticed.
It'll be fine as long as you're careful. Besides...

Who's going to notice a floating pencil way up there anyway?

A floating pencil? Where?
Uh—

What the—? A floating pencil?! Everyone, look!
It's a floating—
Aerem compositum nunc resolvo!

Where?
BOOP
I don't see any floating pencil!
I wanna see it!

But— but I swear there was a pencil floating there...

This is why nobody likes you, Anna. Or you, uh, uh— new kid.
Weirdos!

Zachary! We've spoken about disrupting dining hall before, and—
They started it!
And I'm ending it. Now return to your table, Zachary!

Here's the truth, the "hand on my heart and hope to die" honest truth...

Maybe I **was** a little worried about coming to America. Just a little.

New school, new country, new everything— and, it turns out, worse magic.

There was a part of me that thought I might not pull it off this time. That I'd finally run out of tricks. But now...

Now I know things might just work out after all.

Chapter Three:
In which things absolutely do not work out after all.
Xx Yy Zz
That's Ms. Kayla with the umbrella. She's my homeroom and history teacher. That means I see her every day, whether I want to or not.
Settle down, class. You too, John.
And I am one thousand percent certain she hates me.
READ

Now then, last time we'd just started looking at early American history.

Can anyone tell me some of the people who were on the *Mayflower*?

Yes, John?

I had to endure fifty minutes of that before the period was over.
Almost an hour of **this**...
Yes, John?

And **this**...
Let's all see if John knows the answer!

And **this**.
HISTORY
John, your answer, please?

She hates me.
Oh, she ***definitely*** hates you.

I'm at sixes and sevens about it, Anna! Normally people *like* me, and if they don't, I've at least given them a good reason!
My patented charm has *never* backfired like this before.

I'm not surprised—
Ms. Kayla used to be nice, but this year—gah. You wanna be in her good books.
Sorry, Kid.

But I haven't even *done* anything to her! It's like she took *one* look at me and just decided to—to definitely hate me forever for *no reason.*
Welcome to my world.

But this isn't what normally happens to me, Anna! People *like* me.
I'm not used to it like *you* are!

Wow.
Tell me more about your "patented charm," Constantine.

READ
I didn't mean it like that, I—
Kid, I know you're excited to discuss trigonometry with your fellow mathematicians-in-training, but please refrain until class is over.
Now, continuing from yesterday...
Let's look at some consequences of the Pythagorean theorem.
Dear Anna,
I made a shambles of things, and I'm really sorry. Ms. Kayla riled me up. I didn't mean it and I didn't mean to take it out on you. I said something stupid because I'm not used to having friends but truth is I think you're great, and I like you, and I think people who don't like you are muppets.
Can we be friends again?
Here's the spell I used to connect the surface of my paper to yours. If you use it too you can write me back:
→ Commuta facies chartarum nostrarum ←
-Kid

Commuta facies chartarum nostrarum.
First off, we'll be learning about some trigonometric functions.

These relate an angle in a right-angle triangle to— what?

The ratios of the lengths of the two sides?
Correct.

Now, this may seem like I'm going off on a ***tangent...***
skrtch skrtch

Commuta facies chartarum nostrarum.
That was a pun, children. I assure you, by the end of this class you will understand just how hilarious it is.

Kid:

Look, just make sure it doesn't happen again. I said we can be friends if you don't lie to me, but you also have to not be a jerk. If you can do those two things...

Then yes, friends. :)

-A

Thank you, Anna.

You're welcome, Kid.

Now then: math is just a series of puzzles—and what must we do to solve something we don't understand?

Investigate it?

Correct. Remember that, students: there's not a problem out there that won't crumble in the face of sustained, logical investigation.

Kid,

Oh my gosh I just had the best idea. (Okay I'm totally stealing from Ms. Bravo but still.) We should investigate Ms. Kayla! We're magic, we can actually do this! She'll never know it's us and we can each use our new magic skills to find out what's going on! It's the best idea ever! Do you agree it's the best idea ever? ☐ yes ☐ no

"Yes" is the correct answer,

-A

I'm adding another checkbox beside "yes" and "no."
Oh?
For "um, *absolutely?*"

Kid, this is going to be <u>amazing</u> and also <u>awesome</u>

Agreed!

We are literally magic and can summon pencils and magically unlock small locks and that's more than most kids or even most <u>actual detectives</u> can do!

I drew how this is gonna go:

Haha yes, we will talk at lunch

First we need to learn about <u>triangles</u>

Now, given all that, does anyone know what $\sin^2 x$ plus $\cos^2 x$ equals?

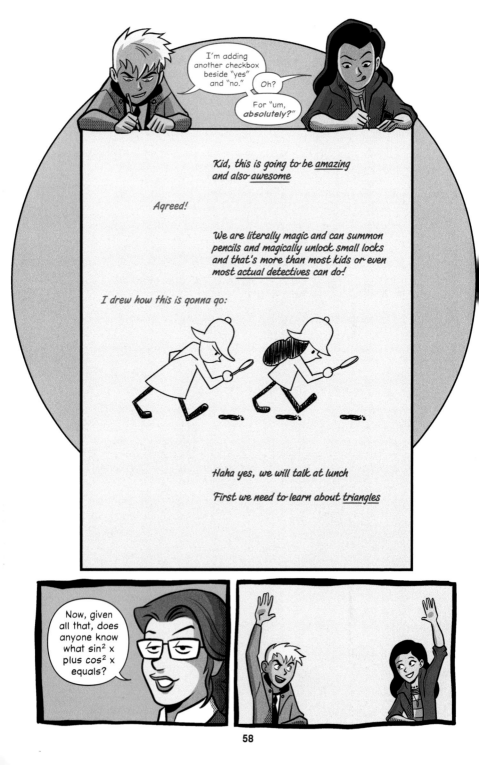

Another advantage of being unpopular at school...
So here's the plan: tomorrow Ms. Kayla's taking us on a field trip. Just to the woods next door, but still. We begin our investigation then.
You can scheme in the dining hall and everyone's too busy ignoring you to listen in.

Ms. Kayla will be busy outside getting everyone organized, which gives **us** our chance to sneak in and go through her stuff.
Ace. What are we gonna nick first?

Johnny! We're not **stealing** anything. We're just **looking.** For **clues,** Kid.
All right, all right, we'll play it your way.

But I really don't think we'll find a piece of paper that says **"Why I Hate Everyone but Especially Kid Constantine, by me, Ms. Kayla."**
No, but every investigation has to start **somewhere,** Johnny, and ours obviously starts with her.

TAP!
Then it's sorted. Tomorrow at nine, Anna...
You and I are going to solve the **mystery** of the **meanest teacher.**

Okay, let's go over this once more. Everyone has their buddy, yes?
klik

THE DOOMBOUND CODEX
FORSAKEN SPELLS
-BY AND FOR-
THE WITCHES OF DARKNESS
Ms. Kayla...
Is an actual, real-life *witch.*

No way. ***No way.***
Witches were the only ones who ever ***made*** books like this. I don't even want to know what kind of ***skin*** it's bound in.
We're snookered here, Anna.

Even the dodgiest witch was more powerful than ***any*** other magic users—including us.
Plus they're ***famous*** for killing children. This school would be like a ***buffet*** for one.
But I thought witches were fake. Just stories.

Like magic and lock-toggling spells?
Touché.

I'd heard they'd emigrated to America after Columbus "found" it.
After Salem, they disappeared. They've been presumed extinct for centuries.
See? You do know ***some*** history.

Only about magic. We're in deep, Anna. Witches were the last dark-magic users, and when they were at their peak...
Well, nobody could stand against them.

So here's my plan.
I can't open it, Kid.
We take the book. We bring it to the principal. Maybe the cops.

Must be a protection spell. I can't budge it either!
Course, they won't believe us at first, but when they lay their peepers on a book that literally crackles with evil energies, it should go a long way to convincing them.

Without it, though, we've got nothing. So as long as we can take this book **before** Ms. Kayla notices we're missing...we're golden.
Pull harder!
I'm pulling as hard as I can! Come on, we need to grab it before Ms. Kayla notic—

klik
And just like that...

Before Ms. Kayla notices ***what,*** children?

Our last chance is gone.

John. Anna. You shouldn't be here. You're supposed to be outside.

What could've brought you into my room, I wonder?

cough cough
Muta statum pessuli.
cough

But Anna handles it **brilliantly.**

Locked!

Ah, so it is. No matter.
There're no lozenges in there, Johnny.

That sounds like a bad cough. Run down to the nurse's office, then meet the other students outside. After all...

We don't want any of my students getting *hurt,* now do we?
No ma'am thank you ma'am.
We'll do that, miss, thank you, miss, goodbye, miss.

Later...
Now, monsters aren't usually covered in history class, but as people in the past did believe in them, so long as you don't write to your parents about this... we should be fine.
Haw!
We're going to learn about American cryptids, dating back to colonial times.
Imagine moving here, to a place you call "the New World"...and you know nothing. You don't know what's safe to eat.
You don't even know what lives on this continent.
But you've heard stories. Stories of magic...
And monsters.
Listen to her! Is she toying with us?
Maybe she heard me cast the locking spell?
I have no idea!
Do you think she caught me closing the drawer?
I did the magician's trick of waving with one hand to distract her while I closed it with the other one, but you never know if it worked!
This whole thing is insane! She could be onto us right now!
What does she want?!

Of course, these days we know that magic and monsters don't ***really*** exist, but nobody did back then.
They let their imaginations run ***wild.***

Wait! That umbrella—does she always carry it?
Yeah, every day, even when it's sunny.
She told us it's good to be prepared, but—

Oh my gosh. Witches and water. ***She can't get wet,*** or she'll ***melt.***
Exactly.

This area of the world—perhaps these very woods—was home to ***dozens*** of supernatural beasts, invented by those first colonists and those who came after them.

Bigfoot, chupacabras, and ***things*** that lurked in the ***swamp.*** They were uniquely American monsters...
And your ancestors went to their ***graves*** believing they stalked these very grounds.

Is that true? Do those exist?
I don't know! I only know European things—Nessie, that sort of stuff! I don't know if what she's on about is **real,** but—
And they didn't stop there.

These colonists soon began to see **witches** everywhere. They were terrified of something more **powerful** than their muskets—so they did the only thing they knew how to do, the only thing that came naturally to them.
They tried to **murder** every one they found.
But they could never be certain they got **all** of them.

They could never know if one of these powerful creatures had **escaped** their clutches, **survived,** and **never forgotten** what **humanity** had **done** to them.
Isn't that right, **Johnny?**
GULP

Now, how many of you have ever seen something you couldn't explain?
She knows. She's **definitely** toying with us, Johnny.
Right. We need to get out of here. **Now.**

What?! John, we can't just *run.*
She's a *witch,* Anna! That's *exactly* what we should do: run to *safety!*

But what about the others? If Ms. Kayla's a threat, then she's a threat to *everyone,* not just us!
We have a moral obligation to stay and help our classmates!

Help them? Anna, they *hate* us and they wouldn't lift a finger to help us. If anything, they—
Ah. Anna and John.

Perhaps you'd like to share what you're discussing with the class?

EVERYONE, RUN! SHE'S A WITCH! MS. KAYLA IS A WITCH!
GET AWAY FROM HER NOW OR WE'RE ALL DEAD!

FEND FOR YOURSELF! GET AS FAR AWAY AS POSSIBLE!

THERE'S NO TIME, MATES! IT'S ALL TO POT! GET OUT OF HERE NOW!

Ms. Kayla is definitely going to kill me.
If I was back across the pond I could maybe try fighting her, but this is her turf. There's nothing I can do to stop her, and she knows it. So, I guess it turns out this diary is really just the story of how I died.
I guess all diaries are like that, if you take a long enough view.
Chapter Four:
In which an infernal being is discovered...
And things go from bad to worse...
To very bad...
To very much worse.

I know you're new here, John Constantine.
And I know that can be hard.

But that doesn't excuse your behavior today. Nor does it excuse your trying to drag another student down with you.

I don't know how they did it back in England, but here at the Junior Success Boarding School, we respect our teachers.
And you will respect **me.** Because I'm not a "witch"—
I'm your **friend.** Or at least, I'd like to be.

I know I have a..."reputation" with the other students. Of it, I will say only this: you can't control what others say about you, only what actions you take yourself.
I encourage you, John, to make better choices.

Yeah, she's good.
She's **real** good.

She gives me the chance to think, "Wait...**have** I been imagining this?"
I know you'll do better, John.

You're excused. There's still some free time before dining hall. Go have some fun.
Okay?
After all, Anna and I only saw some weird book in a locked drawer. I haven't any **actual** proof of **anything.**

Maybe she's just fond of umbrellas. Maybe she simply collects rare books. Maybe we got overexcited and imagined the dark energy. Maybe this **is** all in my head.
Oh, and one more thing.

Yes?
Like I said, she's good. Ms. Kayla gives me just the briefest taste of hope...

And then she **burns** it right in front of me.
Don't cross me again, Constantine.
ARRRGH! MY ARM! MY ARM'S ON—
Fire?

Kid! There you are! I'd just about given up hope of finding you!
How'd it go with Ms. Kayla?

Fine.
Fine? Come on, you've got to give me more than ***that.***

It was fine, Anna. Everything's fine. I don't want to talk about it.
Well, did she admit to being a ***witch?*** Did she say what she wants? Did you get any clues? Did she—

I said it was fine!

I'm done eating anyway.

My parents always told me the most important thing to know in the world is yourself. Who you are, what you want, that sort of thing.
Well, I know who Kid Constantine is.
And I'll tell you this much, mate: he's not a **hero.**
But he's not anyone's fool either. He's smart enough to know when he's **beat,** smart enough to know that you don't mess with **witches...**
And he's **definitely** smart enough to know when to **run.**
It's nobody's fault. There's heaps of schools in America, and it's just my rubbish luck to get the one with a witch.
Once I'm escaped from here, I'll ring my parents and get them to send me somewhere else.
Anywhere else.

THUD

THUMP

And yeah, I glance back. Because I want to remember this place as it was. Because I know the next time I hear about it—whether on the news or through some schoolyard rumor...

SMAK!
It's definitely not going to be **good.**

GAAAH!

Anna! You scared me half to death, love! What are you doing here?!
Stopping you, clearly. Running away, are we?

After the way you behaved at dinner, I figured Ms. Kayla had you good and terrified. I just knew you'd do something stupid like this! I knew it.
Oh, this isn't stupid. This is smart.
When the going gets tough, Anna, the tough get going.

What?!
I don't know how they did it in England, but in America that expression means "the tough get working," like on solving the problem!
It doesn't mean they run away!

You can come with me! You should come!
We can find someplace new, and—
I have a life here, Kid. Like you do.
What, with those other kids? Come on. They hate you! They hate both of us!

Yeah, probably. But they're still living beings. They're human. And I'm not abandoning them to be gobbled by some history-teaching witch.
No matter how completely bonkers that sounds.

Is that why you came to America? Did things get too "tough" in England, so you bailed on the whole country?
Yes, okay? **Yes.** And I'm not **apologizing** for that. It was **dangerous** there, just like it's now **demonically** dangerous here!

If there's a witch at school, then we have an obligation to **reveal** it, to—to **protect** everyone here!
Anna...
That's what decent people **do!** They look out for each other!

You can't just **bail** on everyone when things get hard, Kid!
Oh, I can, Anna. I absolutely can.

And I'm **real good** at it, too.

Johnny!

Another reason not to have friends...
Nobody to yell at you when you go.

I know, I know: not my proudest moment. And yeah, I'm at my lowest. But I keep reminding myself: Kid, you can't save everyone.
"Ooh, I'm Anna! I think I'm **sooo smart** just because I don't know how dangerous witches are!"
Sometimes the only person you can save is yourself.
"I'm gonna give Kid an ear-bashing just because he doesn't want to get eaten by a witch in some—some **barmy school** filled with people who hate his guts! **He's** the idiot here!"
ARRGH!
And yes, I will admit that it took me over fifteen minutes of angry stomping through the woods before I calmed down enough to realize...
I have **no idea** where I am.

Ostendas mihi viam quaeso!
My locator spell doesn't work, but no problem.
I have a backup spell that summons helpful fairies...
Auxilium voca!
Whiiiiich also fails instantly.
Ostende mihi praesentiam ceterorum!
I cast a basic "reveal life" spell, hoping that it'll at least show me the way back to civilization.
And it actually works! Kinda?
What it shows me is something—unexpected.
What's this then?

Something, I admit, I can't quite explain.

I think to myself, "Kid, the only thing on the outside of this forest is a witch, a call to your parents who are going to be proper furious when they find out you bunked off school...

"And Anna, who I'm pretty sure hates your guts now."

It's not solid. I'm pretty sure what I'm seeing is just the magically revealed outline of—well, whatever walked here.
Easily four times as wide as me. Not human.
Crikey, what did Ms. Kayla say about cryptids?

Chupacabra? No, there'd be spines. And we're too far from any swamps...
That leaves—what did she call it? Large Trousers?

No. Dodgy Toes? Hmm...it sounded more American.
Big—something.
Big Shoes? Big Limbs? Big...

BIGFOOT!

Ahh! The furry beast, not man nor bear?! You must inform me, child: where?

Listen, Mr. Foot, I don't want any trouble, I didn't even know you existed, I'm lost and I don't—
Ah-hah! You think I'm him, and less than man.
You're wrong...behold the demon Etrigan!

Demon?
Did you say Demon?

Cor, what a relief! For a second I thought you were some American cryptid.
You have known fear, but then you see a demon and your relaxation shows.

I will admit, Kid Constantine, this is not how this usually goes.

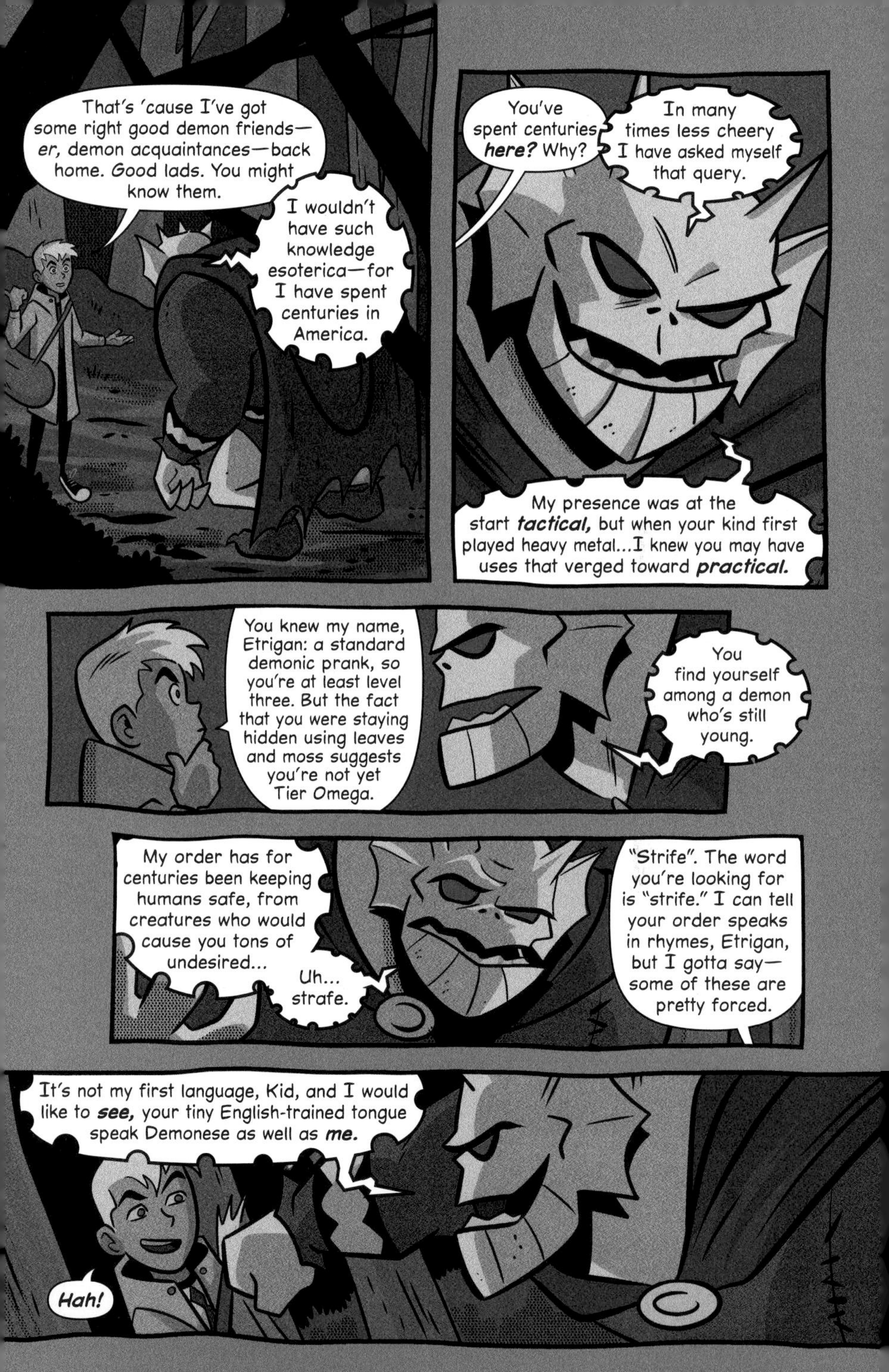

That's 'cause I've got some right good demon friends—*er,* demon acquaintances—back home. Good lads. You might know them.

I wouldn't have such knowledge esoterica—for I have spent centuries in America.

You've spent centuries ***here?*** Why?

In many times less cheery I have asked myself that query.

My presence was at the start ***tactical,*** but when your kind first played heavy metal…I knew you may have uses that verged toward ***practical.***

You knew my name, Etrigan: a standard demonic prank, so you're at least level three. But the fact that you were staying hidden using leaves and moss suggests you're not yet Tier Omega.

You find yourself among a demon who's still young.

So you're a demon whose job is to protect humans from creatures that would kill them, because your order believes we humans have their uses. Love it.

As you may suspect, that summation is correct.

So what kind of creatures are we talking about?

Wolves? Bears?

To stop your boundless guessing, Constantine: I hunt the natural enemy of my kind.

The creatures who have made this land their niche...

I hunt the cursed, dreadful, evil ***witch.***

So it turns out Etrigan's part of a group of immortal demons who saw potential in humans, and came to Earth to protect it against the threat of witches.
It's like with rabbits in our world: get too many of those wee fuzzballs and they'll gobble every leafy green in their path. So you get some coyotes, to keep their population in line.
Rabbits and coyotes, witches and demons.
But what nobody expected was for the rabbits to **level up.**
Nobody thought the rabbits would **kill** the coyotes.
Turns out the demons weren't as immortal as they thought.
Heck of a way to find out.
The demons and witches warred for years, until all the witches were gone... and Etrigan was the only demon of his kind left.
And here on Earth he remained, in the woods of Massachusetts, near where their headquarters had been. A watchful guardian...

Until Ms. Kayla started casting spells this year.
In response to your informed guess, I can only reply with one word: "yes".

And though it has involved sticking out my neck, I have been using some Earthly tech.
You're spying on Ms. Kayla, too? That's perfect! We tried that, but she caught us. All we found was a right evil book locked in her desk.

Yes. I sensed your history when you ventured near, which is why I allowed you to find me here.
Hah! I'm pretty sure you didn't **allow** me to find you, Etrigan. That was all Constantine.

We have to stop her here and now: if she achieves her goals, all mortal life could go kapow. But I have long known: I can't do this alone.
Etrigan...
Constantine, I sense you bend toward "chaotic neutral with a little bit good sometimes, but don't count on it," just like me.

Will you join forces and help me **end** this threat beastly?

No.
I can't, mate.

Ah. I see. You choose instead to flee.
Aw c'mon, you don't need me, Etrigan! You're a tough demon, you can take on Ms. Kayla no problem, yeah?

I say this with a sigh: I have no choice but to try.
Yeah, you got her. Brill.
Hey, let me ask you a favor while you're at it— can you keep an eye out for Anna?

That palindromic name you speak: who is this "Anna" that you'd have me seek?

Oh, she's great. She's actually really, really great! She's about my height, dresses in black, and **super** talented. She's my best fr—
—iend.
Um—I guess she **was** my best friend. My only friend, actually. But the whole thing went a bit pear-shaped.
I don't think she likes me anymore.
John, I will watch out for her safety— that much I can say.
But my understanding of humans still has to go a long way.
Oh? How so?
Why ask me to look out for her if she's someone you no longer care for? And if you care, why leave her behind in the coming witchy war?
Even we demons help those we've liked and known, but you humans apparently **abandon** your friends alone.

I suppose there are things about your kind I will never understand.
Goodbye, John Constantine.
And if you find out who invented heavy metal music, please tell them I think they're grand!

A sick heavy metal riff!

It's hard to admit when you've made a mistake, even to yourself.

Most of us can't do it. Heck, I'm **terrible** at it.
But sometimes, you don't need to do that hard work. Sometimes the answer's just dropped right at your feet.

Sometimes, all you need is for a rhyming demon to look at you...
And tell you **exactly** what he sees.
I'm **not** who Etrigan saw. And I'm **not** going to abandon Anna to her fate.
I'm **Kid Constantine,** dang it.
And I'm going to do **better.**
Etrigan! Wait up! Wait up!

This.
This is the most dangerous place in the universe.
Chapter Five:
In which the world of mortals begins to end.
But I don't have a choice. I'm alone, and there's a monster on campus, and I have to do **something**.

So I do my **best...**
Muta statum pessuli.

And hope that spying on her will reveal something— **anything**— to stop her.
CRRK!

By brimstone and fire, and with hatred's heart...
The walls between our worlds now fall apart!

SHOOM!

pfft!

Good.
Good.

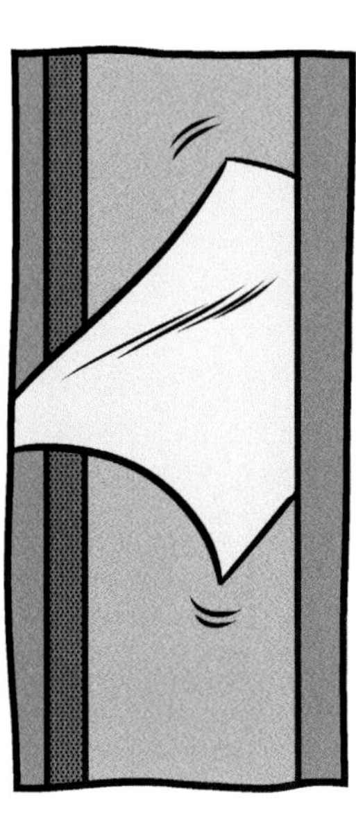

I will say this...

WORLD-ENDING PORTAL ATTEMPT EIGHTEEN

- FULL PORTAL NOW OPEN, BRIEFLY SUSTAINED
- STRENGTH/INTENSITY DEF. RELATED TO MOON CYCLE
- FULL MOON TOMORROW; TREND SHOWS PORTAL WILL REMAIN OPEN FOREVER
- FINALLY! LESS THAN 24 HOURS REMAIN

*It's a heck of a thing to learn that your best isn't going to be **nearly** good enough.*

Oi. That's serious business.
GAAAH!

Kid! What are you doing here?
Would you believe I looked deep inside myself, had a complete change of heart, and came back to apologize to you, stop Ms. Kayla, and as it apparently turns out, save the entire world while we're at it?

Uh-huh. You are a smooth talker. And what brought on this sudden moment of clarity, pray tell?
Well, buddy, I don't think you're going to get a better intro line than that...

Though this was not according to my plan...

Behold the demon Etrigan!

He's real, he's a demon, and he likes humans. Weird things happen around me.
I dunno what to tell you.

Whoa!

Who are you? What's your secret origin? Can I really trust you—or Johnny? What are you doing here? What do you know about Ms. Kayla?
I—
Do you always speak in rhymes? Do you know any spells? Can you shoot demonic fireballs out of your hands?

And then I grilled Etrigan for 45 minutes straight.

And now I've told you all I can, about the demon Etrigan.
I—I do believe you have. Wow.

Shame you can't shoot fireballs out of your hands. That would solve this, no problem.
Such a spell would be quite neat, but past my reach lie magic feats.

Okay, here's the deal. I'm annoyed at **him,** and I'm thrilled to meet **you,** and that kinda evens it out—plus we don't have time to be annoyed at each other anyway.
So this is me reserving the right to be annoyed at Kid later.

For now, I am **much** more interested in teaming up with an actual demon to take down a witch. Cool?
Aces.
Agreed.

So the way I see it, we need to stop Ms. Kayla by tomorrow evening—**before** the moon rises.
Yes: that's when her powers will be at their strongest, and her evil will be at its... wrongest.
You'll get there, bud.

But the question is: **How** do we stop her from opening that infernal portal? She's getting more powerful every second.
And it's not like I have a *"Hey, give the evil witch thing a rest"* spell.
That's kinda why I ran in the first place.

I know, I know. And we've only got less than twenty-four hours until it's game over. But there're still three of us and only one of her!
There must be ***something*** we can do...

Wait. Of course. Of course!
"Of course"? You have a way to stop this witch's force?
It won't be easy...

But yeah.
Yeah, I think I have a way we three could still work a little ***magic.***

I tell them my plan. And just between us, I take back everything bad I ever said about boarding school.
The kids may be mean and the teachers might not care, but when you ***do*** *finally find your people...*

School is ***awesome.***

The next day, Ms. Kayla's class passes normally...
Anna. John. You're ***late.***
I'm sorry, Ms. Kayla.
I'm still learning where all the classes are.

Cor, sometimes I wish I could just ***open a portal*** to get there.
That sure would be something, right, Ms. Kayla?
*Except that Kid and I drop approximately infinity hints that we know **everything.***

Right. Well, continuing from yesterday, can anyone tell me why the first Pilgrims came to America?
It was because of a ***witch hunt,*** wasn't it, Ms. Kayla?

I'm actually not sure if the students noticed anything was wrong. But Ms. Kayla...
That's correct, isn't it, ma'am? A ***witch hunt?***
It's a saying about ***hunting witches?***
Have you ever participated in one, ma'am? Maybe on an unexpected side?

*Ms. Kayla **definitely** did.*

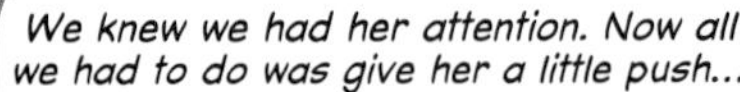
We knew we had her attention. Now all we had to do was give her a little push...

In the direction we wanted her to go.

Ms. Kayla (if that IS your real name),
We know everything. We know your evil plans. And we know: that witch doesn't kill us... only makes us stronger.
Meet us by the big stump in the woods after school at dusk or we tell everyone.
-You Know Who

I got the tape for the note.

John got the fruit from the dining hall.

Because after all, an apple a day...

Brings the witches out to play.
Ms. Kayla (if that IS your real name),
We know everything. We know your evil plans. And we know: that witch doesn't kill us... only makes us stronger.
Meet us by the big stump in

Dusk.
No going back now.

We don't know if Ms. Kayla's here already, so we've agreed not to talk. She could be listening in.

We walk to the stump in silence. And it's weird: in the woods, normally there's always noise.
Animals rustling, birds chirping, that sort of thing. The odd owl hooting.

Today it's dead silent. I don't want to say that it's creepy, but it's definitely not **NOT** creepy.
Johnny and I have agreed to wait here for an hour before deciding she won't show.

Anyway.
Turns out we didn't need to worry about that.

I warned you not to bother me again, John. Now you're going to die.
And look, you're getting your little friend killed, too!

Nice going, hero!

B-before you kill us, c-c-can we just say something?
What could you **stupid** kids **possibly** have to say that would interest me?
Just...
Just...

Just that you did **exactly** what we thought you'd do.
WINK!

Behold the end of all your plans: a bath courtesy of *Etrigan!*
No! **NO!**
NOOOOOOO!
KA-SPLASH!
NO! NO!
Seems to me like ***this*** "stupid kid" knew your weakness, lured you out, ***and has a demon for a friend!***
And we knew where to find a free bathtub, too!
AY, HERE'S THE RUB / I.O.U.: ONE BATHTUB
We're fixing it later!

AAAH! AHHHHHHH!
AHHHHHHHHHHH!

AHHHHHHHH-HAH-HAH-HAH!
HAH HAH HAH!

Anna, are you...?
No, that's not me, I'm not levitating her!

Though she floats above this town, **Etrigan** will bring this witch back **down!**

Hilarious.
SMAK!

You really thought I was a **witch?** Someone whose weakness is **water,** on a planet **lousy** with the stuff?
Let me ask you this, **idiots.** Could a witch...

Do **this?**
SNAP!

FWOOOOOOOOOOMPH!

*Honestly, part of me is pretty certain a witch **could** do this—*
But a bigger part of me knows it's best not to point that out right now.

Witches were **fools,** mere **humans** messing with powers that they couldn't begin to understand.
Ms. Kayla, you—
Take that **name** out of your mouth, **Anna.**
You too, **Constantine.** In the few minutes you have left before your world is ended, you shall address me by my **true** name.
For you are not **only** in the presence of—
But you have interfered with the **plans** of—
And have **earned** the **undying hatred** of—

The dread demon...
X'AOYA!
And in this moment all I can think is one thing, instantly known beyond a shadow of a doubt...
"Anna, you're **definitely** in trouble."

Chapter Six:

In which the underworld is triumphant.

X'aoya, you're a demon! I get along great with demons!

Johnny...

Let's talk about this, X'aoya!

The way I see it, we can eat some candy, have some fizzy drinks, and get this sorted right quick!

X'aoya is one of the most powerful demons in ***history.*** She can easily wipe the floor with you and me.

You should listen to your little friend, John, because unlike you...

Let me be so bold as to say—
We will not die today this way!

Leave them alone, you—you—devil!

You think a pebble will stop me?

Anna's a proper hero. She's bought us some time.
PCHOO!
YIPE!
I don't intend to waste it.

Right. X'aoya isn't the kind of demon I know. I don't think she's one you can make friends with.
She should be in the underworld, for anyone of her tier should not be able to survive up here!
Etrigan gives me the seed of an idea. It's not much—but it's all I have.

Hey, X'aoya! Shouldn't you be **dead?** How come you can survive up here, anyway?
And I'm willing to gamble ancient dread demons like talking about **themselves** as much as regular adult humans do.

Your world is **minutes** away from ending, and you want to know how I can **live** here?
Mortals really are as curious as they are **foolish.**
To answer your insipid question, my kind **is** cursed to be unable to enter the mortal realm, **John.** But I found a way around that...

With a **host.**
Of course: **that's** why Ms. Kayla suddenly became so **mean** this year!

If we can **disable** her host, we might still defeat her before we're toast!
Oh, you'd have to **kill** this poor woman to even **harm** me. And rest assured...**that** is not going to happen.

You know what I'm enjoying the most about this? The idea that you—two *mortal children* and a *lesser demon*—really think you can stop me.
Nothing can stop me.
In a few minutes—just as soon as the moon fully rises—all of Earth will become an *underworld.*

That's your plan? To make Earth into a land of fire and death?
You know how many people live here, child? Do you have any idea? *Seven billion.*

You mortals die so easily, *all the time,* and believe me: we get *more* than our fair share of you down there. But our underworld was built for *500 million, tops.*

And yes, the overcrowding down there works as a great punishment, but after a certain point, it stops being fun.
Quite frankly, we're running out of space down there.

Which is why I'm turning *your* realm into a new overworld for *us.*

So *that's* why you were so *mean* to me—you hate all life up here! You're the reason school's been such a right drag!

Oh, I do hate all life, I really do, but it's more than that.

This was *personal,* John Constantine.

I could *smell* the magic on you.

And because of your influence, soon Anna *reeked* of it, too.

I knew I could use it to draw you out, get you so focused on *me* you'd ignore the bigger picture.

It worked better than I thought...

Seeing how you lured *Etrigan* here, too. You and Anna will die, of course.

But by using *him* as a new host, instead of this puny schoolteacher, your meddling has merely assured that the apocalypse will be that much more dire.

Try it X'aoya, and then you'll see...it won't be so easy to take over *me!*

Etrigan—thank you for the invitation.

I believe I shall.

You just need some ***softening up*** first!
KA-SMAK!

Etrigan can take a blow...

And return it, ***doubled,*** to his foe!

Honestly, Etrigan, the rhyming thing is almost as adorable as you thinking you can beat me.
Don't ever change.

Okay. Cards on the table, Anna: I don't have a plan here.
Johnny, I'm right there with you.
But we have to do ***something.***

What are you thinking?
I'm thinking, if the greatest weapon I have is summoning pencils...

Aerem in peniculum nunc compono!
Aerem in peniculum nunc compono!
Aerem in peniculum nunc compono!

Then I'mma summon me some gosh-darned pencils.

It's like you said, Kid: when the going gets tough...

The tough get going!

YOU!

You—you *dare* to attack *the dread demon X'aoya* this way?

You would *pierce* this host to *nothing?*

Johnny!
It's not enough, Anna! I'm sorry, mate, but *it's not going to be enough!*

KID! YOU CAN'T JUST LEAVE US HERE! YOU CAN'T—

SWOOFH!

Aw, poor baby. At least you've got me incapacitated, right?

FWOOOMPH!
Oh. Wait a minute.

You don't!

Okay, so Johnny's betrayed me. If I live long enough to survive this, I'll feel bad about it later. But right now, the fate of the world's in the balance. I have to do **something.**
Aerem in peniculum nunc compono!

So I do what I can.
Take this, you jerk!

This is getting tiresome.

There's really nothing you can do to harm me, you know.
CHRRRT!

Look: the moon's almost there. With every instant I can *feel* my power growing.
Oof, what did I miss while my consciousness went...

Poof?
There's nothing you can do now but watch the moon rise.
And watch your world *end.*

So this is the moment where the good guys lose. The moment where hope dies. And in the middle of it, all I can think is this...
Say what you will about Kid Constantine, but one thing's for certain—

I sure know how to make an **entrance.**

Oi.

That'll leave a mark.

I knew abandoning us was not what you did. It's good to see you again—
Kid!

Here's the thing, love. Despite my ***and your*** best efforts, I ***have*** made some friends here...
They're two you've got tied up there with—what, the American species of underworld worm-beasts, I'm guessing?

And it made me realize the truth about friendship. It's a simple one.
Anna and Etrigan here—they're my friends because I love them.

And when you love someone, you want to be your best self for them. Just as you want them to be the best selves *they* can be.

You definitely don't want them to **die.**

So a few minutes ago I'm thinking, "*Gosh, I wish there was a way I could* ***be*** *that best self and fight X'aoya.*
"*I wish there was* ***some*** *way I could match her demonic power.*"

Ah, but you can't.
That's right, X'aoya. I definitely can't.

But then I think, hey, even though we weren't friends and even though I didn't give them any reason to, there were still some blokes in England who showed me the kindness of at least **tolerating** me.
They were demons, X'aoya. Old-world demons.
And they told me things.

Like how they were vulnerable to ***salt.***

The levitation spell Anna taught me sends a whole dining hall's worth of salt right into X'aoya's **face.**
Not gonna lie, loves: it's brilliant.
It's right and proper **brilliant.**

ARRGH! No! NO!
NOOOO!

With each attack her worm-strength weakens! It's time to teach her the lesson she, *uh,* seekens!
Of **course.** I should've seen it sooner. All this fire around us—
And X'aoya hasn't even broken a ***sweat.***

It makes sense! Sweat brings ***salt*** to the surface of the human skin, and salt is deadly for her.
Yep! That's why I did this, Anna!

Sure, but we can go even further, Kid! Etrigan doesn't have any salt in his demon physiology, and I'm guessing X'aoya removed it all from Ms. Kayla when she took over...

But, Kid, you and I...

We've got it in ***spades.***

It's over, X'aoya. Me and Constantine are gonna beat you now...
And we're *barely even gonna break a sweat.*

ARRRGH! ARGHGGGHH!

RRRRRRGH!

Well done, Anna.
Hey. You weren't so bad yourself, Kid.

RRRRRRRRRRRRRRRRGH!
What the—?!

RAAAGH!
Hah! You're too late, humans! All you have accomplished is me abandoning my stupid teacher host!
All that work—for nothing!

You see? Not even salt can harm me now! The moon is risen...
And thus your world ends!

Behold! The portal to the underworld!
CHOOOM
Whoa!
By brimstone and fire, and with hatred's heart...
The walls between our worlds now fall apart!
Can we say one thing before the world ends?
Your realm has fallen, mortals! What could possibly be left to say?
Just two words, X'aoya...
Behind you.

From this world, foul demon, you are hereby **banned**—so spoke the demon **Etrigan!**
SMAK!

MUTA STATUM PESSULI!

NOOOOOOOOOOOOOO!

ZOOP!

Etrigan!

Ms. Kayla!

Did—
Did we just win?

Yeah.
Yeah, friends, I think we did.

We snuck Ms. Kayla into the nurse's office.
It was harder that it sounds.
Chapter Seven:
T-BALL
In which our ~~protagonists...~~
In which our ~~champions...~~
In which our heroes are triumphant.

Eugh...
Though I will say that the best part was finding a disguise for Etrigan.
One more I.O.U. note for the pile.
T-BALL

Ms. Kayla? Are you okay?
I—I think so, Anna. How long has it been?

That depends on what day you think it is.
June 26? And who *are* you?

I'm Kid Constantine.
And you've been out of it for almost four months, ma'am.

I have—blurry memories of it. Of being—possessed.
That's—precisely it, actually. You know about X'aoya?

She's been living in my body for months; I ought to. But it's all so unfocused...
Can you tell us the last thing you remember clearly, ma'am?
I was in my home...

I must've gotten something wrong, because I was trying to summon an enchantment to enhance the learning speed of my students...

But instead, all my spellbook accomplished was summoning an ***elder demon.***
And I've been a witch long enough to know that's not the sort of thing you can just ***take back.***

You're a ***witch?!***

I am, children. As far as I know, I'm the last one left.
And I assure you, I'm not a monster.

I'm River Kayla. Etrigan the Witchhunter, I presume.

I must— you can't— I just—
Etrigan, there were good and bad witches in this world, just as there are good and bad people. Everyone owes it to themselves to be the best version of themselves they can be.

As for myself, I teach ***children,*** and like all elementary, middle, and high school teachers, I'm paid ***less than I should be*** to do it.
You and I are on the same side, I promise.

I know there's a history between witches and demons, but those choices—they were made by my great-great-great-grandparents.
We don't have to let centuries-old prejudices determine our relationship to each other unless you want to.
Do we, Etrigan?

River... so it would seem. And I will go to my realm to report what this means...
That the war is over and my mission at an end...
Because from the witches, there's nothing to defend.

The next morning, I decide to do something I should've done a long time ago.
Kid, there's something I want to tell you.

I want to—I want to be myself. I want the world to know the real me.
I—kinda feel like I already do, Anna?
No, see, that's just it.

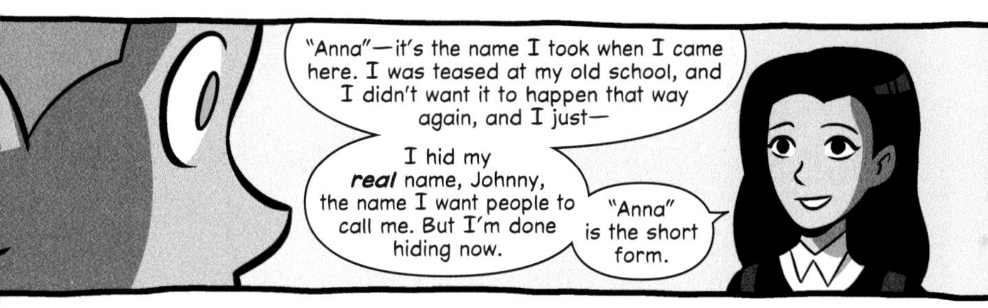
"Anna"—it's the name I took when I came here. I was teased at my old school, and I didn't want it to happen that way again, and I just—
I hid my *real* name, Johnny, the name I want people to call me. But I'm done hiding now.
"Anna" is the short form.

Hi, Kid Constantine.
I'm *Zatanna Zatara.*

Zatanna, that is the *coolest* name I've ever heard.
Thanks. I know some of the kids will think it's weird...

But if there's anything the past few days have taught me, it's that weird is good.
Weird may have just saved the world.

After X'aoya, things have changed. We're actually getting to class **early.**
Knock knock!
It's open!

I'll say this much: it's not what I saw myself doing when I first came here.
Ah, Kid. Anna. Well done. Bright and early, but you're right on time.
It's "Zatanna" now, actually.
Love it.

That gives us the full hour of tutoring before school begins and I wipe this board clean.
Assuming, that is, you're still interested?
Absolutely.
Wouldn't miss it, ma'am.

Excellent. Then let's start at the beginning. Kid, Zatanna: take your seats.
There were a lot of things I thought I knew at the start of this that I now know I didn't.

Now: all magic in the Americas follows its own system of rules, unique from those in the old countries...
In fact, there're a lot of old "truths" I'm not at all sure about anymore. But there is one new one that I **am** certain about.
It's about yours truly: Kid Constantine.

Give me the right motivation—
And the right friends—
And I—**we**—can do just about anything.

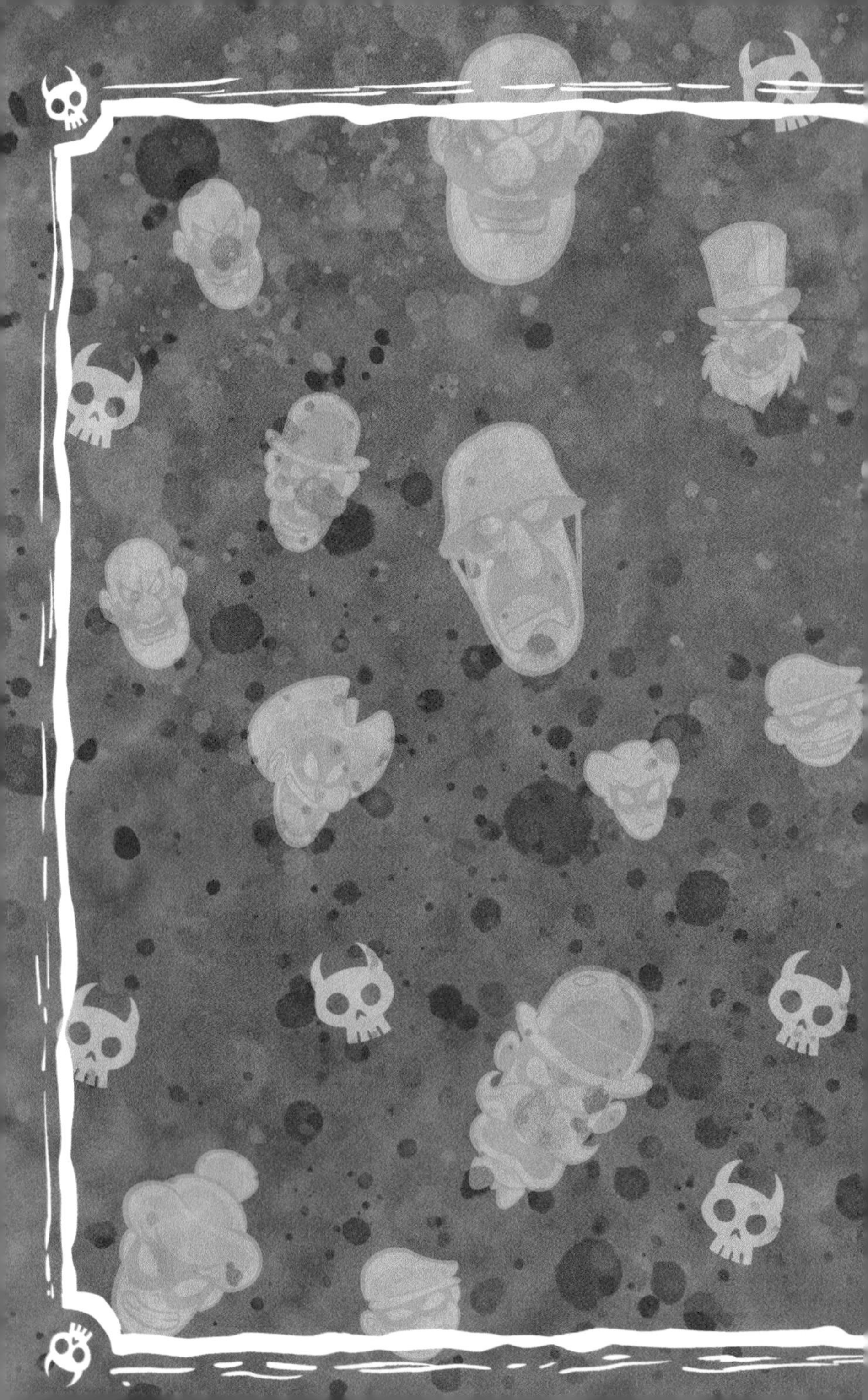

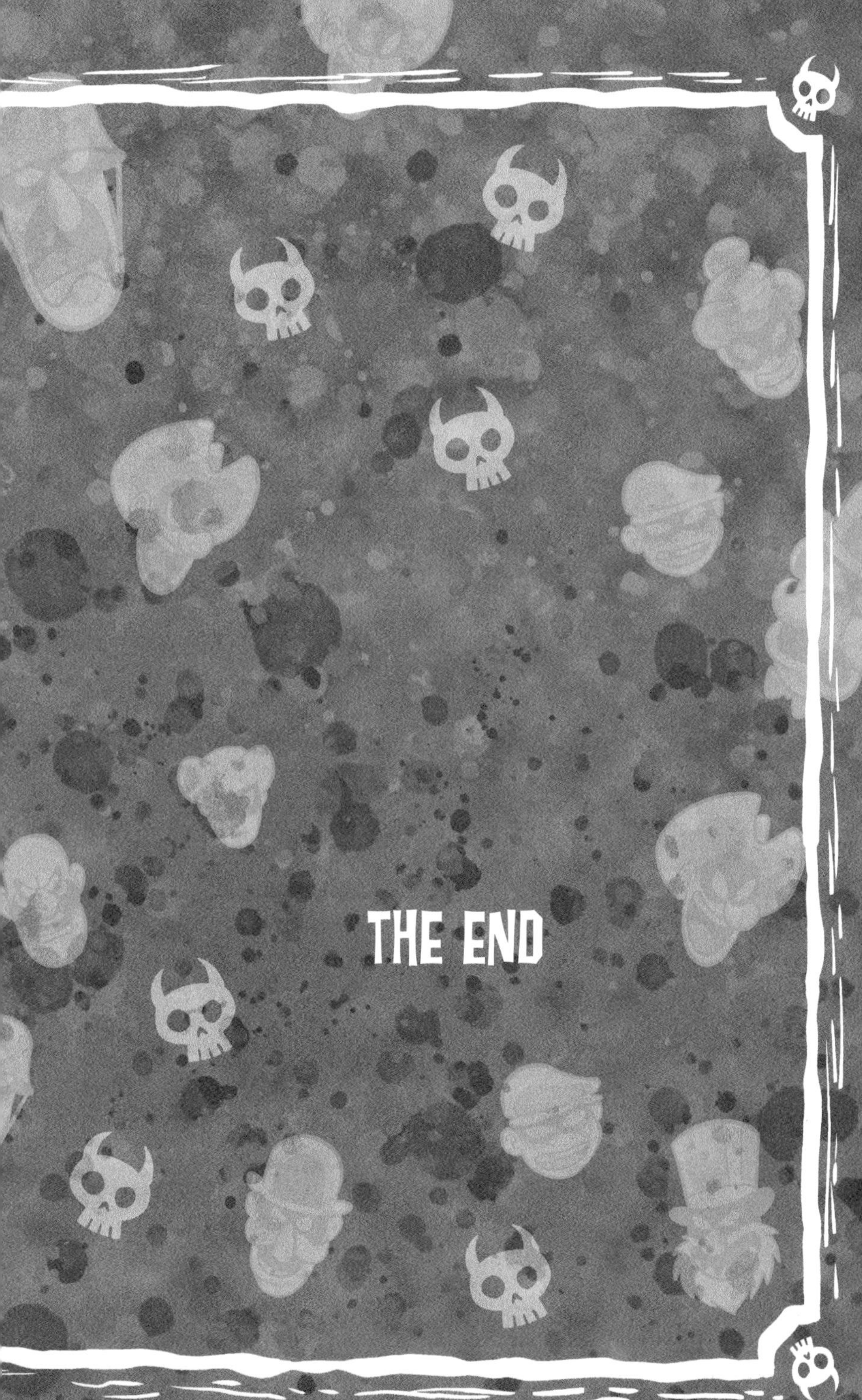
THE END

Some time later...

I'm worried this is about the bathtub. Etrigan said he got that "right on cue, and put back in as good as new," but you never know what that means to a demon.
JANITOR'S CLOSET
Zachary, if this is about your bathtub, I—
It's not about that, Kid.
Wait, how do you know about that?

Uh—
It's not important. Listen, I know this is going to sound crazy, but I think I'm being like—**stalked** by someone. This big hairy guy.

Um, that sounds serious. We can go to the principal, or—
No no, not like that. Like—I keep catching glimpses out of the corner of my eye of something. But only in the woods.
The only proof I have is this one pic.
Snuck it over my shoulder. I know it's not the best, but...

It's the size of his feet that throws me. So what do you think? Can you help me get to the bottom of this?
Yes. Absolutely.
Zachary, you have my undivided attention.
After all, mate...

The supernatural is our specialty.
The end...?

RYAN NORTH is the writer responsible for *Dinosaur Comics*, the Eisner and Harvey award-winning *Adventure Time* comics, the #1 bestselling anthology series *Machine of Death*, and the *New York Times* bestselling and Eisner Award-winning *Unbeatable Squirrel Girl* series for Marvel. He's adapted Kurt Vonnegut's *Slaughterhouse-Five* into a graphic novel, turned Shakespeare into *New York Times* bestselling choose-your-own-path books, and his book *How to Invent Everything* is nothing less than a complete cheat sheet for civilization. He lives in Toronto, where he once messed up walking his dog so badly it made the news.

DEREK CHARM is an Eisner Award-winning comics artist and illustrator living in New York. He was the artist on the *Jughead* and *Jughead's Time Police* comics series for Archie Comics, *The Unbeatable Squirrel Girl* for Marvel, and *Star Wars Adventures* for Lucasfilm/IDW Publishing. Outside of comics, he has done illustration and design work for Random House, Marc Jacobs, and DreamWorks Animation.

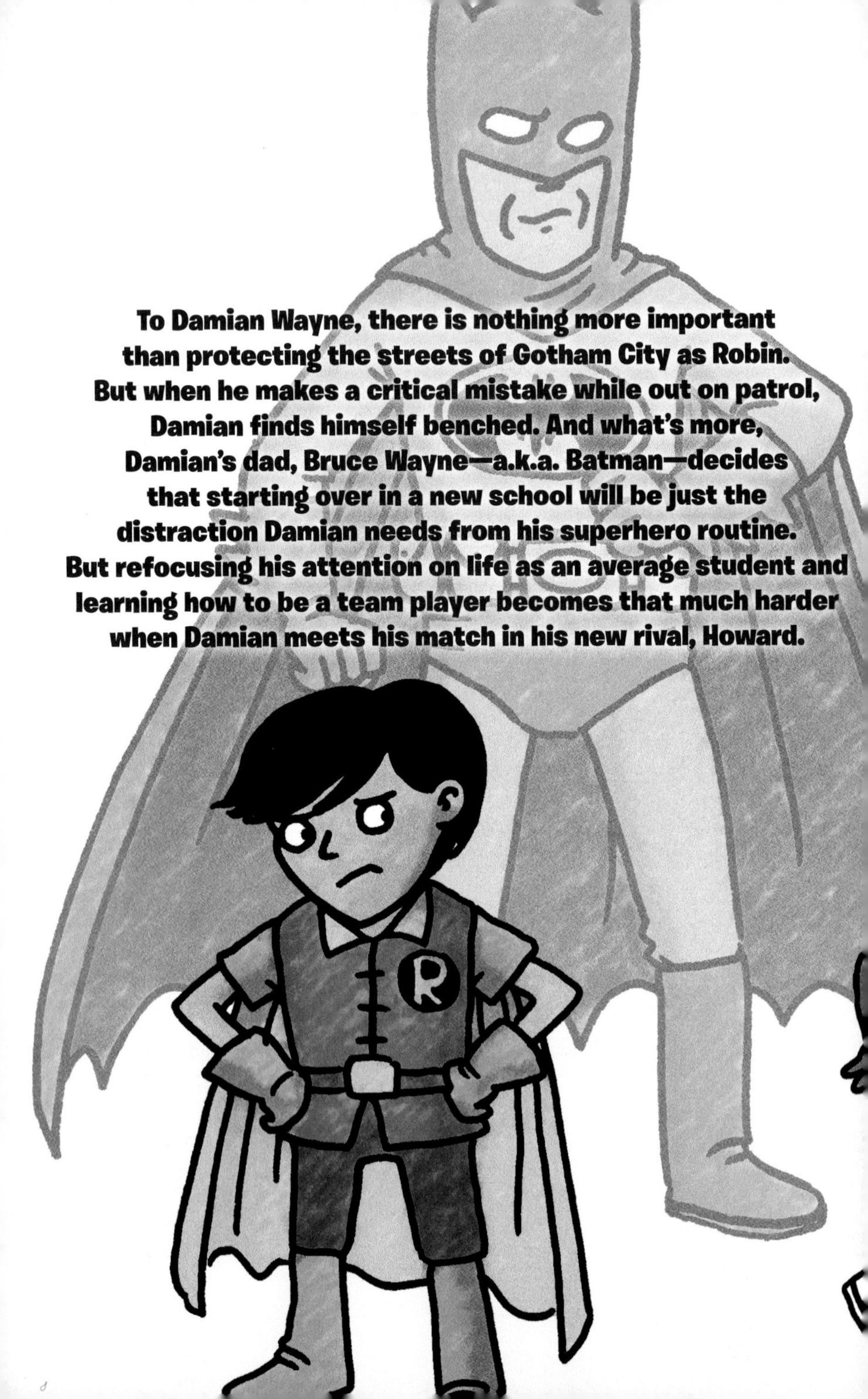

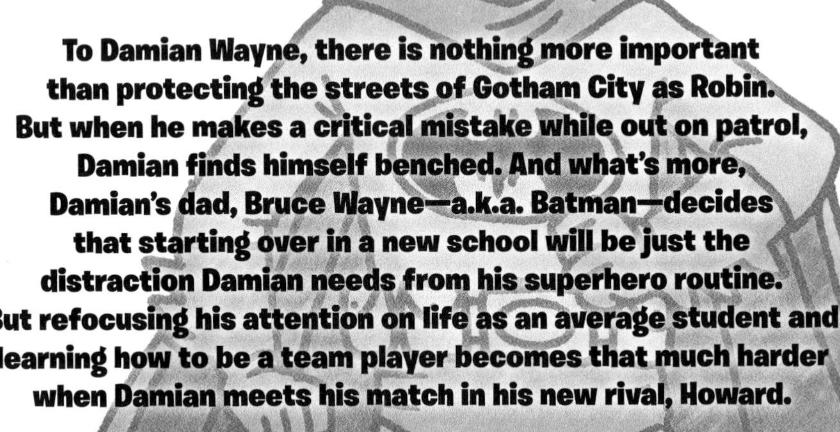

To Damian Wayne, there is nothing more important than protecting the streets of Gotham City as Robin. But when he makes a critical mistake while out on patrol, Damian finds himself benched. And what's more, Damian's dad, Bruce Wayne—a.k.a. Batman—decides that starting over in a new school will be just the distraction Damian needs from his superhero routine. But refocusing his attention on life as an average student and learning how to be a team player becomes that much harder when Damian meets his match in his new rival, Howard.

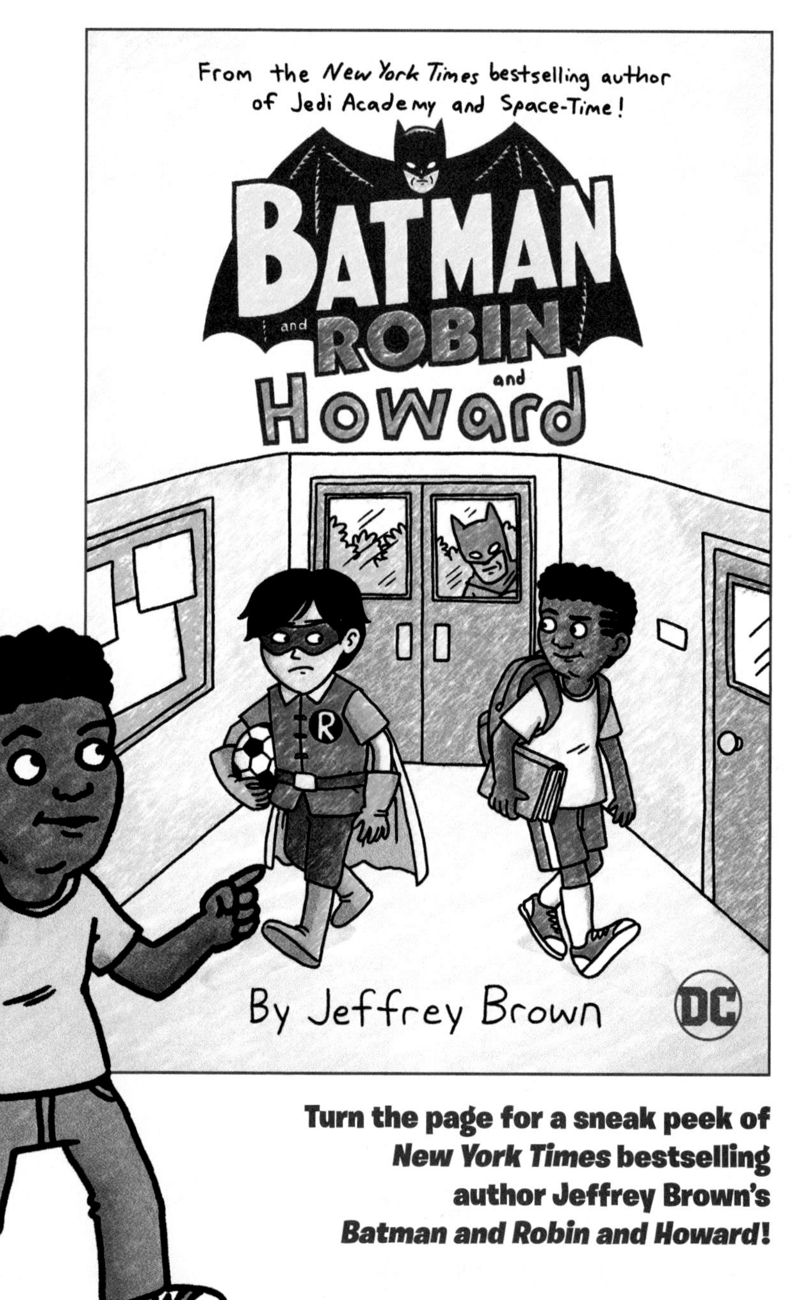

From the New York Times bestselling author
of Jedi Academy and Space-Time!
BATMAN
and ROBIN
and
Howard
By Jeffrey Brown
DC
R

Turn the page for a sneak peek of
***New York Times* bestselling**
author Jeffrey Brown's
***Batman and Robin and Howard*!**

It can be dangerous in this city when it's dark.
Brrrr!
Let's get home quick!

Especially for bad guys.
C'mon, hurry up!
Chill! I've almost got it.

We're going to have to break a window...

You see, I'm—

You can't blame Batman for being a little worried about me.

After all, he is my dad.

Did you hear something?

He can relax, though.
WHUMP!
Let me try.

I'm going to go easy on these punks!
What the—?!

BIFF!
OUCH!

See? Easy!
Ohhh!

AIEEEE! SOMEBODY HELP!

Uh...what?
Uh...
what?
Sorry!
Batman!
Thank
goodness!
Oof!

This will
unlock
your car.
CLICK

Are you okay?
Yeah. The kick
wasn't that hard.
Thanks, Batman.

I'll just stand
over here until
they're gone.

You damaged this other car
when you landed on it. That's
coming out of your allowance.

I'm not upset about losing some allowance, because my real name is Damian Wayne...
...and my dad is billionaire Bruce Wayne.

How was I supposed to know that was their own car and they just locked themselves out of it?!

Observation. Deduction. Patience!

We can't rush into situations based only on how they seem, Damian.

You still have a lot to learn.
Is that why you're making me go to a stupid new school?

I mean, I was already smarter than my teachers at Gotham Prep. What can they teach me at Gotham Metro Academy?

As Alfred once wisely told me, Damian... you don't know what you don't know!

More french fries, Master Damian?
No thanks, Alfred.

I think we're done. Thank you, Alfred.
Very well, Master Bruce.
I'll get my gear.

No patrol for you tonight. Tomorrow is your first day at your new school.
But...

If anyone thinks they know everything they don't, it's my dad.
I'm going to hate this school.

I LOVE this school!
Hello, Howard! How was your weekend?
Good, Elena. How was yours?
GOTHAM METRO ACADEMY

What's up, Javi?
Howsit goin'?

Missed ya, Howie!
HUG!
Aw, thanks, Latasha!

Hey, Azumi! Hey, Pete!
Hey, Howard!

Did you guys hear about Batman this weekend?
Yeah, ridiculous!

I hope at least some of you did the optional extra credit reading, because we're starting with a pop quiz on it!

WHAT?!

See? Easy!

Here you go, Mrs. Goodstein.
Thank you, Howard.

You can read quietly while everyone else finishes.
Can I—

Yes, of course, you may read a graphic novel.
Thanks, Mrs. Goodstein.

BRINNGGGGG!
Okay, kids. Hand in your quizzes.

After lunch we'll work on equations.
What'd you bring for lunch, Latasha?
I'm getting hot lunch today!

How is my veggie burger cold already?
Did you take it from the left side?

No.
You can swap with me. I don't mind.
Thanks, Howard! You're the best.

What's happening?
Everyone's looking out the window.

Let's go see.
Look at that car!
Whoa!
Fancy!

Who's THAT kid?

BATMAN AND ROBIN AND HOWARD
COMING NOVEMBER 2021